FISCHER FINDS
A FRIEND

GARY WEILAND

ISBN: 979-8-9855352-3-5 (paperback)
ISBN: 979-8-9855352-4-2 (hardcover)
ISBN: 979-8-9855352-5-9 (digital)

This book is dedicated to anyone who might look a little different than everyone else. Our differences make us human. Embrace it. Show love to one another and treat them as you would want to be treated.

"GONG! GONG! GONG! GONG!"

The fire station emergency tones were ringing!

"Someone must be in trouble!" said Fischer. "Let's go!"

Fischer and the other firefighters climbed into the fire truck to check out the emergency. Firefighters get called out to different types of emergencies, like house fires, car accidents, or when people are sick or hurt. This was a car accident on Main Street. People were trapped inside the car.

"We better hurry," said Fischer. They flew through town with all their lights flashing, honking the horn. The other cars on the street slowed down, moved to the right, and stopped so the fire truck could go by them safely.

The firefighters got to the car accident and found two cars smashed together. Fischer and the other firefighters hopped off the truck and grabbed some tools. They quickly cut the car doors off and helped the people who were trapped inside. Fortunately, no one was hurt.

ANIMAL SHELTER

While the firefighters were putting their tools back on the truck, Fischer noticed that the accident was right in front of The Animal Shelter. He looked through the large front window and saw a little puppy lying down. The puppy seemed very sad.

Fischer went inside to see the puppy. As he got closer, her tail started to wag and she stood up!

Fischer looked at the worker, Chris, and asked, "Can I pick her up?"

"Sure!" said Chris.

When Fischer picked up the puppy, he noticed something different about her. She only had three legs. One of her front legs was missing.

"What happened to her other leg?" asked Fischer.

"I don't know," said Chris. "I found her outside like that. She's been here for a few months. No one wants to take her home."

We Care

"That's probably why she looks so sad," said Fischer. "I think she would make a perfect pet. After all, I'm missing a leg too. What's her name?"

"She doesn't have a name," said Chris.

Fischer noticed a mark on her body where her leg was removed. "What's that mark from?" asked Fischer.

"That's where she had stitches from her leg surgery. That mark will be there forever," said Chris.

Fischer looked at the puppy. "Stitches, huh?" he said. "Okay, I think I'll call you Stitch. How much does it cost to adopt her?"

"Twenty dollars," said Chris.

Fischer paid Chris and said, "I'll be back to pick her up after I get off work."

Fischer and the other firefighters went back to the fire station. Fischer couldn't wait to get off work and pick up Stitch!

After Fischer got off work, he went straight to
The Animal Shelter. He bought a leash and put it
on Stitch. They walked around the shelter, looking
to buy everything a puppy needs.

He bought her some chew toys, treats, a little doggy bed, food, and puppy pads. They were all set!

On the ride home, Stitch stuck her head out the window and let the wind blow through her fur. She stuck her tongue out and slobbered all over the place!

When they got home, Fischer set everything up for Stitch. He made her doggy bed and gave her a treat. Then they went into the backyard. It was a big backyard! There was lots of room for Stitch to play.

Fischer was curious if Stitch could run with only three legs. She could walk pretty well but running was different.

At first, Stitch was a little shy. This was a new place for her, so she wasn't sure how to act. Fischer grabbed a ball and threw it across the yard. "Go get it, girl!" he yelled with a smile on his face.

Stitch looked at the ball rolling across the yard, looked back at Fischer, barked, and then took off after the ball. She was faster than any other dog he had seen before! Even though she only had three legs, it seemed as if nothing was going to stop Stitch from living her best life.

Fischer knew that Stitch was the perfect dog for him. No one else wanted to adopt her because she looked a little different. Fischer looked passed her difference and saw a puppy that just wanted to be loved like any other puppy.

Fischer looked down at Stitch and said, "I think this is going to work out great. What do you think about going on some adventures together, Stitch?"

Stitch looked up at Fischer and started jumping up and down. She was super happy and couldn't wait for their adventures to begin!

www.ingramcontent.com/pod-product-compliance
Lightning Source LLC
Chambersburg PA
CBHW041006170626
46815CB00002B/189